SADDLEBACK *Classics*

WHITE FANG

JACK LONDON

ADAPTED BY
Janice Greene

SADDLEBACK
PUBLISHING·INC.

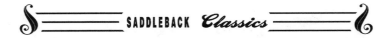

SADDLEBACK *Classics*

The Adventures
of Huckleberry Finn

The Adventures
of Tom Sawyer

The Call of the Wild

A Christmas Carol

The Count of Monte Cristo

Dr. Jekyll and Mr. Hyde

Dracula

Frankenstein

Great Expectations

Gulliver's Travels

The Hound of
the Baskervilles

The Hunchback
of Notre Dame

Jane Eyre

The Jungle Book

The Last of the Mohicans

The Man in the Iron Mask

Moby Dick

Oliver Twist

Pride and Prejudice

The Prince and
the Pauper

The Red Badge
of Courage

Robinson Crusoe

The Scarlet Letter

Swiss Family Robinson

A Tale of Two Cities

The Three Musketeers

The Time Machine

Treasure Island

The War of the Worlds

White Fang

Development and Production: Laurel Associates, Inc.
Cover and Interior Art: Black Eagle Productions

SADDLEBACK
PUBLISHING·INC.
Three Watson
Irvine, CA 92618-2767
E-Mail: info@sdlback.com
Website: www.sdlback.com

ISBN 1-56254-535-3

Printed in the United States of America
08 07 06 05 04 03   9 8 7 6 5 4 3 2 1

CONTENTS

 1 In the Frozen North

A dark forest stood on both sides of the frozen waterway. Silence covered the empty, lifeless land. It was the Wild—the savage, frozen-hearted Northland Wild.

Down the frozen waterway came a string of dogs, pulling a sled. One man walked behind the sled, the other in front of it.

The last pale light of day was fading when they heard the first howl. Then a second howl rose, piercing the silence like a needle. A third howl followed.

"Wolves!" Bill cried. "They're after us."

"Meat is scarce," said Henry. "I ain't seen a sign of a rabbit in days."

When darkness came, the men stopped at the edge of the waterway and made camp.

Bill fed the dogs. Then he asked Henry, "How many dogs we got now?"

"Six," Henry replied.

"Well," said Bill, "I took six fish out of the bag. I gave one to each dog—but I was one fish short."

"You counted wrong," Henry said.

"Nah. I saw the other one run off across the snow," Bill said. His voice was cool and sure. "I saw seven."

"Then you're thinking it was one of them wolves?" said Henry.

Bill nodded.

Howl after howl turned the silence into a madhouse. The sounds came from every side of the camp. The dogs were frightened. They huddled so close to the fire their thick fur scorched in the heat.

A wall of darkness pressed about the men on every side. A circle of glittering eyes had drawn about their camp.

"How many cartridges did you say you had left?" Henry asked.

"Three," Bill said. "And I wish it was three hundred. Then I'd show 'em what for!" He shook his fist angrily. "I wish this trip was over and done with. I wish you and me was asittin' by the fire in Fort McGurry."

Henry grunted and crawled into bed. As he dozed off he was awakened by Bill's voice.

"Say, Henry," Bill said. "That one that came in and stole a fish—why didn't the dogs fight it? That's what's botherin' me."

"You're botherin' too much," Henry said.

Morning came. In the darkness just before dawn, Henry went about preparing breakfast. Bill got the sled ready.

"Say, Henry," Bill suddenly asked, "how many dogs did you say we had?"

"Six," said Henry.

"No, five—one's gone," Bill said.

Henry swore. He left the cooking to go out and count the dogs.

"You're right," Henry said. "Fatty's gone."

"He always was a fool dog," Bill said.

"But even a fool dog like Fatty wouldn't go off and commit suicide that way," Henry said. "I bet none of the others would do it."

After breakfast, the men turned their backs on the cheery fire and went out into the darkness. At once the howls began, the wolves calling out to one another. Daylight came at nine o'clock. It lasted until three o'clock, when the Arctic night fell on the land. The men made camp.

Henry was bent over a bubbling pot of beans when he heard Bill yell. Then he heard a sharp cry of pain from among the dogs. He looked up just in time to see a dim form disappearing across the snow. Bill was standing by the dogs, holding part of a salmon.

"That dern wolf got half of it!" Bill said. "But I got a whack at it just the same. Did you hear it yelp?"

"What'd it look like?" Henry asked.

"Couldn't see," Bill said. "But it's tame, whatever it is. It's comin' here at feeding time to get its piece of fish like the other dogs."

That night, when supper was finished, the circle of gleaming eyes drew in even closer than before.

Bill was nervous. "I wish we was pulling into Fort McGurry right now," he said.

"Shut up your wishing," Henry burst out angrily.

Early the next morning, Henry was

aroused by Bill's loud swearing.

"What's up now?" Henry called out.

"Frog's gone," Bill said.

"No!" Henry cried out.

"I tell you *yes*," Bill said.

Henry leaped out of his blankets and counted the dogs. Then he cursed the powers of the Wild for robbing them of another dog.

After a gloomy breakfast, the four remaining dogs were harnessed to the sled. That day was a repetition of the days that had gone before. The two men toiled without speech across the face of the frozen world.

That night, Bill tied each dog to a stick with a short leather thong to keep them from running off.

Henry nodded with approval. "That's the only way to ever hold One Ear," he said. "He can gnaw through leather as clean as a knife. But now he can't even reach it to chew."

At bedtime, the men heard One Ear making quick, eager whines.

"Look at that, Bill!" Henry whispered.

They watched a doglike animal glide into the firelight! One Ear whined with eagerness

and strained his neck against the thong.

"It's a she-wolf," Henry whispered. "And that accounts for Fatty and Frog. She's the decoy for the pack. She draws out a dog and then all the rest pitches in and eats him up."

The fire crackled. A log fell apart with a loud spluttering noise. At the sound, the strange animal leaped back into the darkness.

"I'm a-thinkin' that must be the one I lambasted with the club," Bill said.

"I reckon you're right, Bill. That wolf is really more of a dog. It's eaten fish many a time right from the hand of man."

"I get a chance at it, that dog is *meat!*" Bill snorted angrily. "We can't afford to lose no more animals!"

"But you've only got three cartridges left," Henry reminded him.

"I'll wait for a dead sure shot," Bill said.

The next morning, Henry shook Bill awake. "Spanker's gone," he said.

"How'd it happen?" Bill groaned.

"Don't know—unless One Ear gnawed him loose," Henry said.

"That cuss!" Bill grumbled. "Just 'cause he couldn't chew *himself* loose, he goes ahead and chews Spanker loose!"

"Tonight I'll tie 'em up out of reach of each other," he said as they took to the trail.

In the cold gray of the afternoon, Henry let out a low warning whistle. Behind them, in plain view, trotted a wolf.

"It's the she-wolf," Bill whispered. "She looks like a big old husky sled dog. Strange color. Looks almost cinnamon."

"Ain't a bit scared," Henry said.

"We've got three cartridges," Bill said.

"But it's a dead shot. What do you say?"

Henry nodded.

But as Bill lifted the rifle to his shoulder, the she-wolf ran off.

"I might have guessed it," Bill cried. "A wolf that knows enough to come in at feeding time would know about shootin'-irons. But I'm going to be laying for her."

"Well, don't stray off too far," Henry said. "If that pack ever starts to jump you, Bill, them three cartridges is worth *nothin'!* Them animals is half-starved."

They camped early that night. Three dogs couldn't drag the sled as far as six. The wolves were growing bolder. They were coming in so close now that the dogs were frantic.

"I've heard of sharks followin' a ship," Bill said. "Well, them wolves is like *land* sharks. They're going to get us, Henry!"

Henry scowled. "They've half got you already, with you talking like that!"

As he dozed off, Henry thought, "There's no mistakin' it—Bill's mighty blue. I'll have to cheer him up tomorrow."

2 Attacked by Wolves

The day began well. They'd lost no dogs during the night, so the men breathed easier. Bill seemed to have forgotten his gloom—even when the sled overturned on a difficult stretch of trail.

It was a bad mix-up. The sled was upside down and jammed between a tree trunk and a huge rock. In order to straighten out the tangle, they were forced to unharness the dogs. The two men were bent over the sled when Henry saw One Ear creeping away.

"*One Ear!*" he called out.

But One Ear broke into a run. The red she-wolf was out in the snow, waiting for him.

When One Ear tried to sniff noses with her, she retreated playfully.

Bill reached for the rifle, but then he hesitated. One Ear and the she-wolf were too close together to risk a shot.

Step by step, the she-wolf lured One Ear farther away. It was too late when One Ear saw his mistake. From every direction, gray wolves now came bounding across the snow, cutting off his path back to the sled. One Ear frantically swerved to the side, the wolves close behind him.

Bill was furious. He started off after them with the rifle. "They ain't going to get any more of our dogs!" he said.

"Be careful!" Henry yelled. "Don't take no foolish chances!"

Henry sat down on the sled and waited. Somewhere out there, hidden by the trees, Henry knew that the wolf-pack, One Ear, and Bill were coming together. It happened all too quickly. He heard a shot! Then two more shots rang out, and he knew the ammunition was gone. Then he heard a great outcry of snarls and yelps. He recognized One Ear's yell of pain and terror. And that was all.

For a long while, he sat on the sled. There was no need for him to go out and see what had happened. He already knew.

At last he wearily stood up and fastened the last two dogs to the sled. He passed a rope over his own shoulder and pulled along with them. At the first hint of darkness, he made camp. After eating, he put his bed close to the fire. The two dogs stayed close by him, one on either side.

Before his eyes closed, the wolves came. Bit by bit, an inch at a time, one wolf would creep forward. Then another wolf would crawl closer, until they were almost within springing distance. At that point, Henry would seize brands from the fire and hurl them into the pack. The wolves would leap back with angry yelps and snarls. Then it would all begin again.

When morning came, the wolves drew back again. Henry was worn out from lack of sleep. After breakfast, he took to the trail. The dogs willingly pulled the light sled. They seemed to know they'd be safe only when they reached Fort McGurry.

The wolf pack trotted along closely now. They were hungry. Henry could see their ribs poking out with every movement.

He didn't dare travel until it was dark. In the last few hours of daylight, he chopped an enormous supply of firewood.

With the night came horror. Not only were the starving wolves growing bolder, but lack of sleep was telling on Henry. He dozed off in spite of himself.

Once he woke to see the red she-wolf less than six feet away. Her mouth opened, and she licked her chops.

Henry felt a spasm of fear in his stomach. He reached for a burning brand, but the she-wolf sprang back to safety.

All night long, he fought off the hungry pack with burning brands.

When morning came, Henry made one desperate attempt to set out on the trail. But the moment he left the fire, the boldest wolf made a leap for him. When Henry sprang back, the wolf's jaws snapped together only six inches from his thigh! To drive them back, he threw firebrands right and left.

That night was like the one before, but now Henry's hunger for sleep was almost overpowering. Desperate to stay awake, he

tied a burning pine-knot to his right hand. When the fire burned his flesh it woke him. For several hours, this worked. Then there came a time when he carelessly fastened the pine-knot too loosely.

Suddenly, several wolves were rushing him at once! They were around him and on top of him. He leaped into the fire. With his hands protected by heavy mittens, he threw hot coals in all directions.

The heat quickly became unbearable. Henry's face was blistering. Yet he still stood near the edge of the fire, throwing burning brands at his enemies.

To cool his feet, he stamped about in the snow. His two dogs were missing.

"You ain't got me yet!" he cried savagely, shaking his fists at the hungry beasts.

Then a fresh idea came to him. He extended the fire in a big circle, and sat in the middle of it. The wolves quickly surrounded the fire, howling their cry of hunger.

Dawn came. The fire was burning low. Now there were some openings in the circle.

The exhausted man sat on his blankets. He felt defeated. "I guess you critters can come and get me any time," he mumbled. "Anyway, I'm going to sleep."

He no longer heard the cry of the hungry wolf pack as they continued their desperate search for meat.

3 One Eye and the She-wolf

At the front of the pack was a large gray wolf. The reddish she-wolf ran beside him. On her other side was an old, one-eyed wolf, wearing the scars of many battles.

A young wolf ran on the blind side of the old wolf. When the three-year-old tried to run closer to the old wolf, a snarl and a snap would send him back.

That day and night, the wolves ran many miles. The next day found them still running. Then, at last, their search was rewarded. They came upon a bull moose!

The starving wolves charged it recklessly from every side. The moose split some of the wolves' skulls with his great hooves. He crushed other wolves and broke still others on his horns. But in the end, there were too many of them. Finally, he went down as the wolves tore savagely at his throat.

Now there was food aplenty. The bull moose weighed over 800 pounds! That meant 20 pounds of meat per mouth.

The fasting was over. Now the wolves were in the land of game. In the days that followed, the pack broke up. Two by two, male and female, they separated from the others.

Now only four were left in the pack: the she-wolf, the big gray leader, the old one-eyed wolf, and the three-year-old.

A fierce rivalry grew among the males. The three-year-old became too ambitious. He caught the one-eyed wolf on his blind side and ripped his ear to ribbons.

Both the leader and the one-eyed wolf attacked the three-year-old. They pulled him down and destroyed him without mercy. Then, as the big gray leader turned to lick a wound on his shoulder, the one-eyed wolf saw his chance. He dove for the leader's neck, his teeth slashing deep.

The leader snarled in outrage, but his snarl quickly broke into a cough. The life faded from him, until at last he lay without moving.

One Eye went to the she-wolf, who leaped and played with him like a puppy. They forgot the tale of love written red in the snow.

In the days that followed, they ran side by side, hunting together and sharing their meat. But after a time, the she-wolf began to grow restless. She seemed to be searching for something she could not find.

One night they came upon an Indian camp. They heard the yelling of men, the scolding voices of women, and the cries of a child. The she-wolf sniffed the scents of the camp with delight. She wanted to go forward, to be closer to the fire. But then she felt the need to go on searching for the thing she could not find. She headed back to the forest.

There they found a rabbit, dangling from a trap. The she-wolf showed her mate how to rob a trap, and they shared a meal.

For two days, the she-wolf and One Eye hung about the Indian camp. Then, one morning, a rifle shot rang out. The bullet smashed against a tree trunk just inches from One Eye's head. The two startled wolves ran off to escape the danger.

They did not go far. For some reason, the she-wolf was getting very heavy and short-tempered. One Eye was patient with her until she finally came upon the thing she'd been looking for. It was a cave near an empty streambank. She went inside and lay down.

One Eye lay down at the entrance. The warm April sun shone on him, and he was hungry. His mate would not leave the cave. At last he went out hunting on his own—but he returned with nothing.

When he reached the cave, he paused at the entrance in sudden shock. Faint sounds were coming from inside! He started forward, but his mate warned him away with a growl. Looking inside, he could see five strange little bundles of life next to her body.

Then old One Eye felt the instinct that came down from the fathers of all the wolves. He knew to obey it. He turned his back on his new family and trotted out on the meat trail.

About half a mile away, he came upon a porcupine. Immediately, it rolled itself into a tight ball of sharp quills. He approached it carefully, but without hope. Once, when he was younger, he had sniffed such a ball of quills. The porcupine had flicked its tail in his face. One quill had stuck in his muzzle. For weeks it stayed there, burning like flame, until it finally worked itself out.

But One Eye also believed in Chance. He came closer to the porcupine and waited. In an hour, though, the porcupine hadn't moved, so he went on his way.

When he was returning to the cave, One Eye saw a large, female lynx. It was crouching in front of the porcupine—in the same place he had crouched earlier that day.

One Eye stayed at a distance from the porcupine and the lynx. Half an hour passed as One Eye watched the game of life being played out before him. The life of one lay in the eating of the other. And the life of the other lay in not being eaten.

At last, the porcupine decided its enemy had gone away. It slowly began to unroll. In that instant, the lynx struck. Its paw shot out at the porcupine's tender belly.

The porcupine squealed in agony. But in the same instant, a single flick of its tail sank sharp quills into the lynx's nose.

The lynx's bad temper got the best of her. She sprang savagely at the thing that had hurt her. The porcupine flicked its tail again. The big cat screamed in surprise and hurt. Now she backed away, sneezing. She brushed her swollen nose with her paws, then shoved it against twigs and branches. Finally, she sprang off yowling.

Once the lynx was gone, One Eye walked slowly up to the porcupine. It had been ripped almost in half, and was bleeding badly.

One Eye was hungry, but he waited until the porcupine's quills drooped and its body quivered. Finally, it moved no more.

He dragged the kill back to the cave. The she-wolf inspected it, then licked him lightly on the neck. She snarled to warn him away from the cubs. But the snarl was not so harsh as before. Now she was less afraid that he was a danger to her cubs. He was behaving as a wolf father should.

4 The Cub's Adventures

One cub was different from his brothers and sisters. Their fur already looked reddish, like their mother's. He was the only gray cub.

Most of his first month he spent sleeping. Long before his eyes opened, he had learned to know his mother by touch, taste, and smell. She was his only source of food and warmth and tenderness.

The only world he knew was the cave. It was small and dark. But one part of the cave was different. This was the cave's mouth—its source of light. From the beginning, he was drawn toward that light. But his mother always drove him back from it.

Like most creatures of the Wild, he came to know famine. There came a time when there was no meat and no milk from his mother. At first the cubs whimpered and cried, but mostly they slept. Yet, while the cubs slept, the life in them was slowly dying.

One Eye was desperate. He ranged far and wide in his hunts. The she-wolf, too, finally left her cubs in search of meat.

Soon the gray cub had only one sister left. When the famine ended, there was food—but it came too late for the sister. As the weeks went on, the flame of life in her flickered lower and lower and then went out at last.

Then there came a time when the gray cub no longer saw his father. The she-wolf knew why he never came back. She followed his trail to the lynx's lair. There she found him, or what was left of him, at the end of the trail.

A lynx is not the kind of animal for a single wolf to fight. But the she-wolf knew there might come a time when she, too, would face the lynx. This she would do for the sake of her gray cub.

By the time his mother began going out to hunt, the cub knew he must not leave the cave. And he knew fear—although he'd met nothing to be afraid of in his young life. His fear was a heritage passed down to him through a thousand, thousand earlier lives.

Once, lying awake, he heard a strange sound at the entrance of the cave. He didn't know a wolverine was standing outside. To the cub, the strange new scent was unknown. Yet he lay frozen with fear. His mother, coming home, growled as she smelled the wolverine's track. Bounding into the cave, she licked and nuzzled the cub. Somehow he knew that he had escaped a great hurt.

There were other forces at work in the cub, and the strongest was growth. Both his mother and fear had warned him away from the mouth of the cave. But one day, fear and obedience were swept away by the rush of life. The cub went out the entrance of the cave.

It was bewildering. The light was painfully bright. Space stretched endlessly before him, making him dizzy.

A great fear came over him. The hair along his back stood up. His lips curled in an effort to snarl. Out of his smallness and fright, he challenged the whole wide world.

Nothing happened. He continued to stare. Soon he forgot to be afraid. He inspected a tree trunk and the grass beneath him. A squirrel running down the tree trunk came right at him. It gave the cub a great fright. But the squirrel was as terrified as he was! This boosted the cub's courage.

He began to walk. At first he was very clumsy. He ran into sticks and rocks. But the longer he walked, the better he walked.

The cub had the luck of a beginner. He fell into the well-hidden nest of a ptarmigan. Seven chicks were in the nest. At first their movement frightened him. He put his paw on one and *made* it move. This he liked! He smelled the chick. He picked it up in his mouth and felt a spasm of hunger in his belly. When his jaws closed, there was a crunching of tiny bones, and a rush of warm blood in his mouth. This living meat was better than the meat his mother fed him! Before walking away, he ate every one of the chicks.

Suddenly, the mother ptarmigan attacked him, beating his head with her wings. He hid his head between his paws and yelped. Then he angrily sank his tiny teeth into one of her wings and pulled hard. The bird struggled against him, beating him with her free wing. It was his first battle—and it made him happy!

The ptarmigan began pecking him on his nose, again and again. He whimpered and finally let go of her wing. But as he started to run away, he felt a rush of air. A hawk, diving down out of the blue, had barely missed him!

Skimming just above the ground, the hawk struck the ptarmigan with its claws. The bird squawked in agony and fright. The hawk flew off, taking the mother ptarmigan with him.

The cub stayed where he was for a long time. He had learned much. *Live things were meat. Also, if living creatures were large enough, they could hurt you.*

The cub was heading back to his mother in the cave when he heard a sharp cry. It was a weasel, leaping swiftly away from him. It was young and very small. The cub turned it over with his paw. The next moment, the mother weasel flew at him. Her sharp teeth cut into the flesh at the side of the cub's neck.

While the cub yelped, the mother weasel and her young one disappeared in the brush.

He was still whimpering when the mother weasel returned. She came closer and closer. Then she leaped—swifter than he could have moved—and buried her teeth in his throat.

The cub struggled to escape. She hung on, pressing down with her teeth to reach that great vein where his life-blood bubbled.

The gray cub would have died if the she-wolf had not come bounding through the bushes just then. The weasel let go of the cub and sprang at the she-wolf's throat. The she-wolf jerked her head like the snap of a whip, throwing the weasel high in the air. As it fell, the wolf's jaws closed on the weasel's body.

The mother's joy at finding her cub was even greater than his joy at being found. She nuzzled him and licked his wounds. Then they ate the weasel and went back to the cave to sleep.

5 Kiche and White Fang

The cub developed a great respect for his mother. She could get meat, and she was not afraid. To him, she represented power.

Famine came again. The she-wolf ran herself thin in her search of meat. Then, one day, she brought home a different kind of meat. It was a lynx kitten. The cub didn't know she had eaten the rest of the kittens in the litter. He didn't know that what she had done was a desperate thing.

After the meal, the cub lay sleeping by his mother's side. He was awakened by a terrible snarl from his mother. Crouching in the entrance of the cave was the mother lynx.

Because of the small entrance, the lynx couldn't leap inside. Instead it made a crawling rush forward. The she-wolf quickly pinned her down. The cub saw little of the battle. But he heard terrible snarling and spitting and screeching.

Once, the cub sank his teeth into the lynx's hind leg. He hung on, and probably saved his mother much damage. When the two mothers separated for a moment, the lynx lashed out her paw at the cub. His shoulder was ripped open to the bone!

The cub cried, but then felt a second burst of courage. At the end of the battle, he was still clinging to one of the lynx's hind legs.

The lynx was dead, and the she-wolf was bleeding and very weak. For a week, she never left the cave, except to get water. By the time the lynx's meat was gone, the she-wolf's wounds had healed enough for her to hunt again.

For some time, the cub limped from the terrible slash he had received. Yet he carried himself more boldly now. He had fought, and he had survived. He had learned the harsh law of meat: *Eat or be eaten.*

One morning, the cub left the cave to drink from the stream. There he saw five strange things. He had never seen such living things. It was his first sight of man.

The cub felt he must run away, but he could not. One of the Indians walked over to him. The cub bared his fangs, and the man laughed as he said, *"Wabam wabisca ip pit tah."* ("Look! The white fangs!")

The man bent to touch him. When the cub sank his teeth in his hand, he received a blow on the side of the head that knocked him over. He sat up and ki-yi'd.

His mother heard her cub's cry. She dashed through the bushes to save him. When she saw him, she bounded forward and snarled at the men.

"Kiche!" one of the men cried out.

The cub was amazed to see his mother, the fearless one, begin to whimper and wag her tail. He couldn't understand. The awe of man rushed over him.

The men surrounded her.

One of them said, "Look! It is a year, Gray Beaver, since she ran away."

Gray Beaver smiled. "It was the time of the famine, Salmon Tongue," he remembered. "There was no meat for the dogs then."

"Aha! I see that she has been living with

the wolves," a third Indian said.

"And this cub is the sign of it," said Gray Beaver, touching the cub. "It is plain that his father is a wolf. There is much wolf in him, and very little dog. His fangs are white, so White Fang shall be his name. He will be *my* dog. For was not Kiche my brother's dog? And is not my brother dead?"

Gray Beaver tied a rawhide string around Kiche's neck.

Salmon Tongue rolled White Fang over on his back and rubbed his stomach. The cub felt ridiculous and helpless, lying there with his legs in the air. It was against his whole nature to be helpless! Yet White Fang submitted to the man's will. And strangely, the rubbing hand felt good. Then Salmon Tongue gave him a final scratch on the ears, and White Fang was no longer afraid of man.

After a time, the rest of the tribe arrived. There were many more men, women, and children—40 of them in all. There were also many dogs. When they saw the cub and his mother, they began to attack. The cub watched as the men struck the dogs with clubs. He heard the animals yelp with pain.

White Fang saw clearly that the will of man was law. And he saw that they enforced their law not with their bodies, but with dead things. They made dead things like sticks and stones leap through the air and bring hurt.

The tribe continued on its march. They came to the end of the valley, where a stream ran into the Mackenzie River. There the tribe made camp. White Fang saw teepees, their flaps moving in the breeze. These frightened him, until he tugged on one and made it move. But then he was driven away by the sharp cry of a squaw. He ran to Kiche, who was tied to a stake in the ground.

A moment later, the cub left his mother's side again. A large puppy named Lip-Lip came toward him, baring his teeth. They circled each other. Then suddenly, with great swiftness, Lip-Lip slashed White Fang's shoulder. White Fang leaped at Lip-Lip, but the big puppy was a better fighter. Again and again, White Fang was bitten. Finally, he ran to his mother, yelping shamelessly. This was the first of many fights with Lip-Lip.

Kiche licked White Fang gently and tried to make him stay with her. But White Fang's curiosity was too strong. A few minutes later, he was watching Gray Beaver, who was doing something with sticks and dry moss. As he watched, something like mist suddenly began to rise from the sticks and moss! Then a live thing appeared, twisting and turning. It was the color of the sun! White Fang knew nothing about fire. He touched his little nose to the flame and licked it.

For a moment, he was paralyzed. Then he

leaped backward, bursting out with ki-yi's. Gray Beaver laughed loudly. When he told the rest of the camp what White Fang had done, everyone was laughing.

White Fang cried and cried. It was the worst hurt he had ever known. Every one of his cries made the Indians laugh louder.

It was then that shame came to him. Now he knew laughter and the meaning of it. He ran to Kiche, the one creature in the camp who was not laughing at him.

As night came on, White Fang lay by his mother's side. He was homesick for the quiet loneliness of the cave. The only life he had ever known had disappeared. Here, in the company of humans, life was always buzzing and humming.

He watched the Indians, moving about the camp. They were creatures of power. They were the lords of the alive and the not alive. They were fire-makers! They were *gods!*

6 White Fang Loses His Mother

The bane of White Fang's life was the older pup. Larger and stronger, Lip-Lip chose White Fang as his favorite victim. Whenever White Fang left his mother's side, the bully was sure to appear and force a fight. Lip-Lip always won.

White Fang could never play with other puppies. Lip-Lip would not permit it. Thus, White Fang was robbed of much of his puppyhood. Instead, he became cunning and his temper grew fierce.

One day, though, White Fang was able to trick his enemy. First, he made Lip-Lip chase him. Usually, White Fang could outrun the older pup. This time, however, White Fang slowed down so that Lip-Lip was only one leap behind. This excited Lip-Lip. He paid no attention to where White Fang was leading him—right to the spot where Kiche had been tied up!

Snarling, Kiche grabbed Lip-Lip with her jaws. She rolled him over so he couldn't run. Then she ripped and slashed him with her fangs again and again. When Lip-Lip finally rolled out of Kiche's reach, White Fang chased him all the way back to his teepee.

The day came when Gray Beaver decided that Kiche would not run off. He untied her and let her run free. Later that day, both mother and puppy walked to the edge of the camp. The woods seemed to call out to White Fang. He longed for the cave, the stream, and the quiet trees. He started to run away from the camp, but Kiche would not follow. To her, the call of the fire—and man—was stronger. When she turned back to camp, White Fang followed her. His need for his mother was stronger than his desire for freedom.

Gray Beaver was in debt to Three Eagles. To pay him, Gray Eagle gave him a piece of cloth, a bearskin, 20 cartridges, and Kiche. Three Eagles was planning a trip to the Great Slave Lake, so he took Kiche with him. Seeing his mother in Three Eagles' canoe, White Fang tried to follow. He sprang into the water and swam after her. He didn't obey when Gray Beaver called him back. He was in terror of losing his mother.

But the gods are used to being obeyed. Angrily, Gray Beaver set out after White Fang in his own canoe. When he caught up with him, he grabbed the puppy by the neck and lifted him out of the water. Then he gave him a beating. And it was a true *beating!* His hand was heavy, and he knew how to hurt.

Finally, White Fang hung from Gray Beaver's hand, crying helplessly. Gray Beaver threw him roughly into the canoe and kicked him out of the way. A moment later, White Fang felt a spark of anger, and he sank his teeth into Gray Beaver's foot!

White Fang's earlier beating was nothing compared to the beating he received now. When Gray Beaver finished with him, White Fang's small body was bruised and sore everywhere. He had learned another lesson: *He must never, never bite the god who was master over him.*

When they returned to camp, Lip-Lip rushed up to White Fang, ready to fight. But Gray Beaver's foot shot out, kicking Lip-Lip a dozen feet away. With that, White Fang learned that the right to punish was reserved for the gods alone.

That night, White Fang cried for his mother. All night he dreamed of the free life that had once been his.

Lip-Lip continued to darken white Fang's days. As a result, White Fang became more and more savage. If there was trouble and fighting in the camp, White Fang was usually at the bottom of it.

One day, he caught one of his enemies alone. He attacked the throat, bit the great vein, and let out the dog's life. The angry tribe demanded vengeance from Gray Beaver. But Gray Beaver kept White Fang in his tent and refused to let anyone punish him.

White Fang became an outcast, hated by both man and dog. The dogs wouldn't let him run with them. But no dog was safe running outside the pack. If one did, White Fang would turn on him and rip him up before the pack could arrive and rescue him.

Sometimes he would lead the pack in a chase through the woods. They always lost him. Their noise would give them away, while he ran like a silent shadow among the trees. Alone and isolated, he was more connected to the Wild than they. He knew more of its secrets. A favorite trick of his was to erase his trail in running water. Then he would hide and listen to his enemies' puzzled cries.

Hated as he was, White Fang never had a chance to learn affection or kindness. His only code was to obey the strong and destroy the weak. He faced constant danger. Because of this, he became faster, more cunning, deadlier, more cruel, and more intelligent than the others. There was no choice. He *had* to become all of these things—or else he would not survive.

7 | The Law of Property

In the fall, White Fang got his chance for freedom. For several days, there was a great hubbub. With the arrival of autumn, the summer camp was being taken down.

White Fang slunk out of camp and hid in the woods. Gray Beaver called him. So did Mit-sah, his son. White Fang trembled with fear, but he did not obey. Finally, the voices died away, and he was alone.

He became cold and hungry. There was no warm side of a teepee to snuggle against. No one threw him pieces of fish and meat. He had forgotten how to fend for himself.

He spent the night lonely and frightened. In the morning, his mind was made up. He followed the Mackenzie River downstream, looking for the trail of his gods.

He did not rest. But his body was like

iron—it paid no attention to fatigue. By the end of the second day, he'd been running for 30 hours. He was weak from hunger now. His feet were bruised and bleeding and he had begun to limp.

Gray Beaver had planned to cross the Mackenzie that night. But his squaw, Kloo-kooch, had seen a moose. Gray Beaver killed it with a lucky shot from his rifle. If this hadn't happened, Gray Beaver would have crossed the river, and White Fang would have passed by without finding his master. He would either have died or found his wild wolf brothers and become one of them.

As White Fang limped along, he smelled a fresh trail in the snow. He followed it, whining eagerly. Finally, he saw the campfire! In front of the fire, Gray Beaver squatted, chewing on a chunk of tallow.

White Fang expected a beating. He crawled to his master's feet, waiting for a blow to fall. Instead, Gray Beaver broke off a chunk of tallow and gave it to him!

That night, White Fang lay at his master's feet, secure and content. He knew that he would not be alone in the forest tomorrow. He would be with his gods.

In December, Gray Beaver went on a journey up the Mackenzie. Mit-sah and Kloo-kooch went with him. Gray Beaver drove one sled himself, pulled by dogs he had traded for or borrowed. Mit-sah drove another sled. This one was pulled by seven puppies, including White Fang and Lip-Lip.

Like his father, Mit-sah was wise. He had seen the way Lip-Lip tormented White Fang. Before, he couldn't do anything about it. But now Lip-Lip was *his* dog. He put Lip-Lip at the head of the team. This would seem to be an honor—but it was not.

Because Lip-Lip was in front, it seemed that he was always running away from the rest of the dogs. As the team chased him, the dogs began to hate him. Sometimes, Mit-sah would give meat only to Lip-Lip. This made the other dogs furious.

Lip-Lip became an outcast, just as White Fang had been. White Fang could have become the dogs' leader, but he was too solitary. He ignored the other dogs, or fought with them. None of them dared to rob White Fang of his meat. Instead, they ate quickly, knowing that the wolf-cub might take it away from them.

As the months passed by, Gray Beaver continued on his journey. Pulling the sled had greatly increased White Fang's strength. Now completely grown, he still saw his world as a cold and brutal place.

He respected Gray Beaver, but he had no real affection for him. The Indian never spoke kind words. That was not his way. His hand was never soft or kind.

In a village at the Great Slave Lake, White Fang learned even more cruelty from the hands of men. He also came to modify one of the laws Gray Beaver had taught him: *Never bite one of the gods.*

In the village, a boy was chopping frozen moose-meat with an ax. Some small chips of meat were flying onto the snow. White Fang had started to eat them when the boy came after him with a club.

White Fang was furious. He knew that he'd done no wrong. Before the boy knew

how it happened, White Fang ripped one of his hands wide open!

White Fang realized that he had broken a law of the gods. He ran to Gray Beaver. Soon the boy and his family arrived, demanding vengeance. But they went away unsatisfied. Gray Beaver had stood up for him.

So White Fang learned that there was a difference between his own gods and other gods. He did not have to be treated unfairly by the other gods.

Before the day was over, White Fang was

to learn more about this law. The boy who had been bitten and his friends followed Mit-sah into the woods. Hot words were spoken. Then all the boys attacked Mit-sah. White Fang leaped into the fight. Five minutes later, the boys were crying and running away. Many were dripping blood in the snow as they ran.

When Mit-sah told his story in camp, Gray Beaver ordered that meat be given to White Fang. In that way, White Fang learned the law of property. What belonged to Gray Beaver must be defended. To do this, he could even bite other gods. Gray Beaver now trusted White Fang to guard his property.

As the months went by, the covenant between man and dog grew ever stronger. The terms of the covenant were simple: From his master, he received food and fire, protection and companionship. In return, White Fang guarded his master and his property, worked for him, and obeyed him.

White Fang's dependence on his master grew very strong. If he ever met Kiche again, he would leave her to go with his master.

8 White Fang Gets Revenge

It was April when Gray Beaver finished his journey and pulled into the home village. White Fang was now a year old. His standing in the world of dogs was not the same.

He realized this change in an encounter with an older dog, Baseek. When White Fang was younger, he always cringed if Baseek showed his fangs. But one day, Baseek tried to take meat away from him. Instead of cringing, White Fang fought back. He struck without warning, and ripped Baseek's right ear to ribbons. Baseek was shocked and bewildered at how fast White Fang had moved. To save his dignity, the older dog walked calmly away from White Fang. He did not lick his wounds until he was out of sight.

In midsummer, a new teepee appeared in the village. When White Fang trotted up to investigate, he found Kiche. He remembered her vaguely. She did not remember him at all. She lifted her lip in a snarl. It was not her fault that she had forgotten him. A wolf mother is not made to remember her cubs of a year before. Now, she had a new litter of puppies to protect. She drove White Fang away with her bared teeth.

The months went by. White Fang grew stronger, heavier, and more compact. He also became more solitary and more fierce. Gray Beaver prized him more every day.

In the third year of White Fang's life, a great famine came to the Mackenzie Indians. The fish failed. Other game became scarce. Driven by hunger, the gods ate the leather of their moccasins and mittens. Then they began to eat their dogs. The weakest were sacrificed first. The other dogs looked on and understood. A few of the boldest and wisest animals ran away to the forest. One of these was White Fang.

He had more experience in the wild than most dogs. Soon he became skillful at stalking whatever animal he could find. One day in the forest, he unexpectedly met Lip-Lip. Like White Fang, the older dog had run away. But Lip-Lip was weak from hunger and White Fang was in perfect condition. In an instant, White Fang struck his old enemy on the shoulder. Lip-Lip went over onto his back. Then White Fang's teeth drove into Lip-Lip's scrawny throat. In seconds, his old torturer was dead.

A few weeks later, White Fang came upon a village near the Mackenzie River. How could it be? It was the old village come to a new place. And now he could smell fish in the air! White Fang came out from the forest and trotted into camp. He headed straight to the teepee of Gray Beaver. The famine was over, and he was with his god once more.

Now White Fang was made the sled dogs' leader. The dogs hated him bitterly, and he hated them in return. If they had been able, they would have killed him. But he was too quick for them, too formidable, too wise. He would have killed them, too, if they hadn't learned to keep together. He might knock a single dog off his feet, but the pack would be on him before he could kill.

In the summer of 1898, Gray Beaver traveled to the Yukon. News of the gold rush had reached the Indian camp. Gray Beaver had brought furs, mittens, and moccasins to sell to the gold hunters. He had expected good profits. In his wildest dreams, his profits were no more than 100 percent. As it turned out, however, his profits were 1,000 percent. He settled down to trade.

It was in Fort Yukon that White Fang saw his first white men. To him, their power was superior to that of the Indians. When he was a puppy, the Indian teepees seemed proof of great power. But the white man's houses, and the huge fort made of logs, showed even greater power.

But if the white gods were all-powerful, their dogs did not amount to much. They were all shapes and sizes. None of them knew how to fight.

Every two or three days, a steamer would arrive, bringing more white men and more dogs. White Fang and a gang of Indian dogs would attack and kill as many as they could.

First, White Fang would pick a quarrel with a dog. This was easy, since White Fang was part wolf. When dogs saw him, they rushed at him. With lightning speed, White Fang would roll them off their feet. Then he would retreat, knowing that white men carrying clubs would come running before the gang finished off their victim.

While White Fang worked with the gang of Indian dogs, he kept himself apart. As always, the other dogs feared him.

If Lip-Lip had not robbed White Fang of his puppyhood, he might have grown up differently. He might have become more doglike and been attracted to other dogs. If Gray Beaver had been an affectionate master, White Fang might have been gentler. But none of these things had happened. White Fang had become lonely, unloving, and ferocious. Sadly, he had become an enemy of his own kind.

 # Two New Masters

Only a small number of men lived in Fort Yukon. They looked down on the newcomers and enjoyed seeing them come to grief. They especially enjoyed seeing White Fang and his gang go after the newcomers' dogs. But there was one man who liked it even more than most. This man was called "Beauty."

No one knew his real first name. But Beauty Smith was anything but a beauty. He was a small man with a little pointy head. His jaw was huge. In some people, such a jaw might mean fierce determination. But Beauty Smith was a coward.

The men at the fort were afraid of Beauty Smith. His cowardly rages made them fear a shot in the back or poison in their coffee.

This was the man who looked at White Fang and wanted to own him. Gray Beaver told him White Fang was not for sale—not at *any* price. But Beauty Smith visited Gray Beaver again and again. Under his coat, he carried a bottle of whisky. Soon Gray Beaver developed a thirst. He wanted more and more of the fiery liquid. His money began to go, and finally it was gone. Again Beauty Smith talked to him about buying White Fang. This time, he offered to pay in bottles, not dollars. And this time, Gray Beaver agreed.

The bottles were delivered. Gray Beaver tied a leather string around White Fang's neck and handed it to Beauty Smith. But when Beauty Smith pulled on the thong, White Fang rushed at him. The brutal man had been waiting for this. He swung his club and smashed White Fang to the ground.

White Fang didn't rush a second time. One smash from the club showed him the white god knew how to use it. But that night, he bit the leather in two and trotted right back to Gray Beaver. Even though his master had betrayed him, White Fang was faithful.

In the morning, Beauty Smith came and took him away from Gray Beaver. Then

White Fang got his worst beating ever.

A few days later, sober and broke, Gray Beaver left to return to the Mackenzie. White Fang stayed at Fort Yukon. He was now the property of a man who was more than half mad. The wolf-dog knew nothing of madness. He only knew he must obey this new master.

Beauty Smith penned White Fang and teased him cruelly. Before, White Fang had been an enemy of his own kind. Now he became the enemy of *all* creatures.

One day, a number of noisy men gathered around White Fang's pen. Then, a huge dog, a mastiff, was pushed inside. White Fang leaped with a flash of fangs that ripped the dog's neck. The mastiff growled hoarsely and dove back at White Fang. But White Fang was here, there, and everywhere. He slashed and leaped away before the enraged mastiff could reach him.

The men outside shouted and applauded. Beauty Smith was delighted. Right from the start, there was no hope for the mastiff. He was too heavy and much too slow. Finally, the mastiff's owner dragged his dog to safety. Bets were paid off, and silver money clinked in Beauty Smith's hand.

There were more fights in the days ahead. White Fang came to look forward them. He had been taught to hate. Fighting was the only way he had to satisfy that hatred.

Then Beauty Smith took his dog on a steamboat to Dawson. White Fang now had a reputation as "The Fighting Wolf." Men paid 50 cents in gold dust just to see him.

A man named Tim Keenan arrived in the land. The first bulldog ever brought to the Klondike was with him. The dog's name was Cherokee. It was inevitable that this dog and White Fang would fight.

The day of the fight, men gathered around White Fang's pen and made their bets. Then Cherokee was put inside. He charged White Fang on his short, bowed legs. White Fang struck. Cherokee whirled around to face him, but White Fang wasn't there! This happened again and again. White Fang would always slash and jump away before the bulldog could bite. But there was a problem. White Fang could not get at Cherokee's throat! The bulldog was too short. As it was, trying to knock the bulldog over, White Fang lost his footing for an instant. At that moment, Cherokee went for his throat.

White Fang was frantic. He couldn't get loose from the deadly jaws. He whirled and turned and slashed until he was exhausted— but Cherokee held on. It was hard to breathe. The men who had placed money on Cherokee raised their bets.

Just then, a dogsled with two men pulled up. One man wore a mustache. The other was younger, and tall.

White Fang's eyes were beginning to glaze over. Beauty Smith could see that the fight was lost. As he began to kick his dog savagely, the tall newcomer broke into the ring. Beauty Smith was about to deliver another kick when the young man's fist smashed into his face. "You beast!" he yelled. With a second blow, he smashed Beauty Smith into the snow.

The tall man bent over the dogs. "Come on, Matt," he said to the man with the mustache as he tried to pull the bulldog's jaws apart.

"You won't get 'em apart that way, Mr.

Scott," Matt said. He took his gun and shoved it between the bulldog's teeth.

The men in the crowd started to protest. But when Scott looked up and glared at them, they went silent.

"You *beasts!*" Scott again exploded before going back to his task.

Tim Keenan came through the crowd and touched Scott on the shoulder. "Don't break them teeth, stranger," he said ominously.

Scott looked at him coolly. His gray eyes were like steel. "You get out of my way," he snarled. "I'm busy."

Matt and Scott gently pried with the gun. Finally, White Fang was pulled free. Cherokee struggled against them.

"Take your dog away!" Scott ordered Tim Keenan. "Get him out of here!"

Matt stooped over White Fang. Beauty Smith got up and came over, too.

"Matt, how much do you think a good sled dog is worth?" Scott asked.

"Three hundred dollars," Matt said.

"And how much for one that's all chewed up?" Scott asked.

"Half of that," Matt answered.

Scott turned to Beauty Smith. "Mr. Beast," he said, "I'm giving you a hundred and fifty for your dog."

"I ain't selling," Beauty Smith snorted.

"Yes, you are," Scott insisted, "because *I'm* buying. The dog is mine."

Scott sprang toward Beauty Smith, who cowered down. "A man's got his rights," Beauty Smith said in a whiny voice.

"That's correct," Scott agreed as he passed him the money. "But you're not a man— you're a beast."

The crowd started to break up then. Tim Keenan turned to one of the bystanders. "Who is that?" he asked.

"Weedon Scott," the man said. "He's one of them mining experts. If you want to keep out of trouble, steer clear of him. The Gold Commissioner's a special pal of his."

"I thought he must be somebody," Keenan said. "That's why I kept my hands off him."

 **A Gentle Voice**

White Fang pulled at the end of his chain, snarling at Weedon Scott's sled dogs.

Scott watched for a while and shook his head. "It's hopeless. The dog is part wolf—he'll never be tamed," he said sadly.

Matt smiled. "Wolf or dog, he's been tamed already," he said.

"No!" Scott cried out.

"I tell you *yes*. And he's been broke to the harness. See those marks across his chest?" Matt pointed out.

"You're right," Scott admitted, shaking his head. "It's still hopeless. We've had him for two weeks now. He's wilder than ever."

"I've got an idea. Why not turn him loose for a spell?" Matt suggested.

Armed with a club, Matt unsnapped the chain and stepped back. White Fang was confused. He watched the gods warily.

"Poor devil," Scott murmured. "What he needs is some show of human kindness." He brought meat from the cabin and tossed it to White Fang, who studied it suspiciously.

Just then, one of the other dogs, Major, made a spring for the meat. In an instant, White Fang knocked him off his feet and dove for his neck. Major staggered to his feet, as blood spouted from his throat.

Then there was a leap and a flash of teeth. Now Major lay in the snow, gasping his last breaths. Matt examined his bloodied leg.

"I told you it was hopeless," Scott said in a discouraged voice. He took out his revolver. "It's the only thing to do."

"Look here, Mr. Scott," Matt objected. "It served Major right. Why, I wouldn't give two whoops for a dog that wouldn't fight for his own meat. Give the poor devil a fighting chance. If he don't deliver the goods, I'll kill him myself. There!"

Scott put away his revolver. "All right," he said. "Let's see what kindness can do for him."

He walked over to White Fang, speaking

gently. White Fang was suspicious. He had just killed the man's dog! Surely he'd be punished. The man's hand came slowly toward his head. White Fang knew the hands of the gods, and how they could hurt. He snapped with the quickness of a coiled snake.

Scott cried out in surprise, pulling his torn hand to his side.

Matt dashed to the cabin and came out with a rifle.

"Don't!" Scott cried. "You begged for a chance. Well, *give* it to him, then! We've only just started. We can't quit now. It served me right this time. Just look at him!"

White Fang was now about 40 feet away, snarling—not at Scott, but at Matt.

"Well, I'll be goshswoggled!" Matt cried.

"Look at his intelligence," Scott said. "He knows the meaning of firearms as well as you do. Put up the gun."

Matt leaned the rifle against the woodpile. As he saw this, White Fang quieted down and stopped snarling.

"I agree with you, Mr. Scott," Matt said. "That dog's too intelligent to kill."

One day later, Scott came up to White Fang again. White Fang growled, expecting punishment. Instead, Scott sat several feet away and talked to him in a soothing voice.

The hair rose on White Fang's neck. But the god made no hostile movement. In spite of himself, the strange gentleness of the voice touched the wolf-dog's heart.

Then the god held a piece of meat in front of White Fang's nose. When White Fang refused to touch it, Scott tossed it in the snow. The wolf-dog's eyes never left Scott as he swallowed it whole.

The god tossed several pieces of meat. Then he refused to toss the meat, but held it out in his hand. White Fang hesitantly approached the hand. Growling a warning, he finally took the meat.

Now the god's hand was coming near his head! The voice continued, soft and soothing. White Fang growled. But he did not snap or spring away. The hand touched him. It was the will of the god, and he obeyed.

The hand patted him. White Fang was wary. At any moment, the hand might grab and hurt. But the god kept petting his head with long, soothing strokes.

It was the beginning of the end for White Fang. It was the end of his old life, the end of hate. A new and better life was coming.

White Fang soon grew to like Scott. He didn't run away, even though he was free. His dependence on man was fixed. As the days went by, the liking he felt for Scott became love. When he was away from Scott, an emptiness filled him.

White Fang slowly adjusted to his new way of life. He learned that he must not kill his master's dogs. And when Scott harnessed him to the sled, he pulled willingly.

In late spring, a great trouble came to White Fang. He became sick while his master was on a trip. In a letter to Scott, Matt wrote, "That wolf won't work. Won't eat. All the dogs is licking him. I'm sure he wants to know what has become of you—and I don't know how to tell him."

Finally, Scott returned. As he stepped inside the cabin, White Fang came up to him, his eyes shining.

"Holy smoke!" Matt cried. "Look at him wag his tail! Always said that wolf was a dog!"

White Fang quickly recovered from his illness. A couple of days later, Scott's sled dogs came after him. But now that his master was back, White Fang had recovered his old power. In a few minutes, the dogs were retreating from his fangs.

The night of Scott's return, he and Matt heard snarling—and human cries.

"The wolf's nailed somebody," Matt said.

They rushed outside. There, in the snow, lay Beauty Smith. His shirt was ripped, and his arms were slashed terribly. Scott pulled White Fang away. The snarling wolf-dog quieted down at a word from Scott.

Matt gave Beauty Smith a shove. Without a word, he went off into the night. In the snow lay a steel dog chain and a club.

"Trying to steal you, eh!" said Scott. "Well, well, he made a mistake, didn't he, boy?"

At Scott's voice, White Fang's growl softened and became contented.

11 Off to California

White Fang could sense it. Something terrible was about to happen. He started to whine as he listened to the gods talking inside the cabin.

"Listen to that, will you!" Matt cried. "I believe that wolf's onto you."

Weedon Scott looked over at Matt. His eyes were almost pleading. "But I *must* leave him behind," he said. "What would I do with a wolf in California?"

"You're right," Matt agreed.

Then came the day when White Fang saw his master packing. He knew his god was going away. That night, he howled for hours.

Inside the cabin, the two men had just gone to bed.

"He's gone off his food again," Matt remarked from his bunk.

Weedon Scott grunted in reply.

"From the way he carried on when you left before," Matt went on, "I wouldn't wonder if he up and died this time."

"Oh, shut up!" Scott snapped.

The next morning, two Indians came and carried off Scott's luggage. Then Scott called White Fang into the cabin.

"You poor devil," Scott said softly as he gently rubbed White Fang's ears. "I'm hitting the long trail, old man. I'm going where you cannot follow. Now give me a growl—a last goodbye growl."

But White Fang refused to growl. Instead, he listened to the steamboat tooting on the Yukon River.

"There she blows!" Matt said. "Be sure and lock the front door. I'll go out the back."

The men walked down the hill to the steamboat *Aurora*. They were shaking hands near the gangplank when they saw him. White Fang was standing several feet away—on the deck of the steamboat.

"Didn't you lock the front door?" Matt demanded.

"You just bet I did," Scott said.

Scott called White Fang to his side. Now he could see the cuts on his muzzle and the gash between his eyes.

"We plumb forgot the window," Matt said. "He must-a busted clean through it!"

The *Aurora* gave one final toot. "Goodbye, Matt," Scott said. "About the wolf—you don't have to bother writing to tell me how he's doing—"

"What!" Matt exploded. "You don't mean to say—"

"Exactly! *I'll* write to *you* about him."

Matt crossed the gangplank just before it was hauled in. He watched Weedon Scott waving a last goodbye. Then Weedon bent over White Fang, smiling and rubbing his ears. "Now, *growl*, you!" he ordered.

Days later, the *Aurora* dropped anchor. Scott and White Fang stepped out onto the wet streets of San Francisco. White Fang was appalled. The streets were crowded with dangers—wagons, carts, and huge horses! Worst of all were the cable and electric cars. To him, they screeched like lynxes! White

Fang was bewildered by the thunderous noise and the endless rush of the streets.

But San Francisco lasted no longer than a bad dream. White Fang was put in a baggage car by his master. When he was taken out, the nightmare city was gone. Now he was in the Santa Clara Valley. Before him was rolling green countryside, streaming with sunshine.

A carriage was waiting. A man and a woman approached the master. The woman's arms grabbed the master around the neck! Seeing the hostile act, White Fang instantly became a snarling demon.

Scott quickly grabbed the wolf-dog and calmed him.

"It's all right, Mother," Scott said soothingly. "He thought you were going to hurt me." Then he spoke to White Fang. "Down with you!"

White Fang lay down reluctantly. As Scott hugged his parents, he kept a watchful eye on White Fang.

There was more trouble when the carriage arrived at Sierra Vista, Scott's father's place. They'd just entered the grounds when a huge sheepdog came running up. Because it was a female, White Fang's instinct prevented him from attacking her. But the sheepdog, whose name was Collie, had no such instinct. To her, White Fang was a wolf, a sheep killer. She sprang on him furiously. White Fang dodged her teeth as well as he could.

Then, a deerhound came bounding up and struck White Fang on the side! White Fang whirled around to attack. But Collie saved the hound's life. Before White Fang's jaws could reach the hound, she knocked him off his feet. The next moment, Scott took hold of White Fang and his father called off the deerhound, who quickly obeyed.

Scott turned to White Fang. "Come on, you wolf," he said. "You'll have to come inside. There are lots of things for you to learn. It's just as well you begin now."

12 Adapting to Civilization

Long ago White Fang had learned that he had to adapt in order to survive. So adapt he did. He soon made himself at home at Sierra Vista. The deerhound quickly accepted White Fang. Had the deerhound had his way, they would have become friends. But White Fang preferred to be left alone.

Collie, however, would not leave him alone. She picked on White Fang constantly. When he saw her coming, he would walk away. Sometimes a nip on his hindquarters made him retreat quickly.

There were many persons White Fang had to learn about. There was his master's father, Judge Scott, and the judge's wife. There were the master's two sisters, Beth and Mary. There was the master's wife, and his children, Weedon and Maud, who were four and six.

White Fang soon learned that all of these people were valuable to his master. Gradually, he grew to like them—especially Judge Scott and the children. But when his master was around, no one else existed.

Outside the house, there was more to be learned. One morning White Fang came upon a hen that had escaped from the chicken yard. White Fang made two bounds. In a flash of teeth, the bird was gone.

Later in the day, White Fang spotted another chicken near the stables. One of the grooms rescued it with a whip. At the first cut of the lash, White Fang reacted by leaping for the man's throat.

Collie saved the man's life. With her teeth bared, she rushed at White Fang while the groom escaped to the stables.

"White Fang will eventually learn to leave chickens alone," Scott said. "But I can't teach him that lesson until I catch him in the act."

Two days later Scott had his chance. He came out on the porch where the groom had laid out 50 dead chickens. He watched White Fang as the wolf-dog watched the chickens.

Then Scott held White Fang's nose down to the dead hens and cuffed him firmly.

Judge Scott shook his head. "You can never cure a chicken killer," he said sadly.

Weedon Scott disagreed. He challenged his father to a bet. "I'll lock him in with the chickens all afternoon," he said. "For every chicken he kills, I'll pay you one dollar in gold."

Hidden out of view, the family watched the performance. But it was a fizzle. Locked on the porch, White Fang lay down and slept.

White Fang learned quickly and well. Cats, rabbits, and turkeys he must leave alone. But when he was out in the fields, chasing a jackrabbit was allowed.

But Collie never forgave him for the chicken-killing episode. Even after he learned these lessons, she followed him around like a policeman. If he even looked at a pigeon or chicken, she burst out in angry barks.

With the exception of Collie, things went well for White Fang. As the months passed, he flourished like a plant in good soil.

There was no real work for White Fang at

Sierra Vista. His most important task was to keep his master company while he went out on horseback. One day, a big jackrabbit rose suddenly under the horse's feet. As the horse swerved violently, Weedon Scott was thrown from the horse's back and broke his leg. He called White Fang to his side.

"*Home! Go home!*" he commanded.

White Fang knew the meaning of home, but he did not want to leave his master.

"*Home!*" This time the command was sharp, and White Fang obeyed.

The family was on the porch in the cool of the afternoon. White Fang arrived, panting. He knocked the children out of the way and stood before Judge Scott, growling fiercely.

"Go away! Lie down, sir!" Judge Scott commanded.

White Fang turned to Scott's wife. He took her dress in his teeth and tore it as she screamed with fright.

"I hope he's not going mad," Scott's mother said. "I was afraid this warm climate wouldn't be right for an Arctic animal."

Then White Fang burst out barking and

they finally got the message.

"Something has happened to Weedon!" the judge's wife cried out.

Now they were all on their feet, running down the steps after White Fang.

After this event, White Fang found a warmer place in the hearts of everyone at Sierra Vista. Even the groom he'd attacked had to admit that he was a wise dog—even if he was part wolf.

As White Fang's second year at Sierra Vista came on, he made a strange discovery. Collie no longer bared her teeth at him. Now there was a playfulness about her nips.

One day she led him off on a long chase into the woods. It was the afternoon the master was to ride, and White Fang knew it. But there was something in him deeper than all the lessons he had learned. It was even deeper than his love for the master. The master rode alone that day.

In the woods, side by side, White Fang ran with Collie. It was just as his mother, Kiche, had run with old One Eye, so many years ago.

§13 White Fang Recovers

About this time, the newspapers told of a daring escape from San Quentin prison. Jim Hall, the runaway convict, was a ferocious man. First, he'd been treated very cruelly by society and then treated unfairly in prison. He'd become a mad beast.

The warden said it was impossible that Jim Hall had escaped. But the cell was empty. Three guards lay dead, their weapons gone.

Farmers hunted him. The law hunted him. Those who encountered him were killed or wounded. And then Jim Hall disappeared!

In the meantime, the news stories were the talk of Sierra Vista. Judge Scott wasn't worried, but the women were afraid. In his last days before retiring, Judge Scott had sentenced Hall to 50 years in prison.

Judge Scott didn't know that the police

had conspired against Hall or that the man was innocent. And Jim Hall didn't know that Judge Scott was merely ignorant. He had threatened Judge Scott with revenge. Then Hall had gone to prison—and escaped.

Alice, the master's wife, shared a secret with White Fang. Each night, after Sierra Vista had gone to bed, she got up and brought White Fang in to sleep in the big hall. Early every morning, she let him out before the family was awake.

One night, while all the house slept, White Fang woke up and lay very quietly. A strange god was in the house! The strange god walked very softly, but White Fang heard him.

Now the strange god was climbing the stairway toward the master and his family! Without warning, White Fang sprang onto the man's shoulders. He buried his fangs in the intruder's neck.

Sierra Vista woke up to angry snarling and growling, followed by revolver shots. Then a man's voice screamed.

Weedon Scott and his father soon stood staring at the man on the floor.

"Jim Hall!" Judge Scott cried out. Father and son exchanged a look.

White Fang, too, was on the floor. As the men knelt over him, he tried to wag his tail, but he could not.

"He's all done in," Scott muttered.

"We'll see about that," said the Judge as he started for the telephone.

The doctor worked through the night. At dawn, he announced: "One broken leg and three broken ribs. Three bullet holes clear through him. He hasn't a chance!"

White Fang proved him wrong. All of his life he'd tended the soft humans of civilization. But White Fang himself had been toughened in the Wild, where the weak die early. He was built of iron.

For weeks, White Fang was like a prisoner, bound up with plaster casts and bandages. Unable to move, he slept long hours. His dreams were haunted by the awful electric cars he had seen in San Francisco.

Then came the day when the last bandage and cast were taken off. All of Sierra Vista gathered around. White Fang tried to rise to his feet, but fell from weakness. He felt ashamed, as if he were failing his gods. Then he made a heroic effort, and at last he stood.

"The Blessed Wolf!" the women cried.

"Yes, Blessed Wolf, indeed," the judge agreed. "And from now on that shall be my name for him."

White Fang slowly limped out into the sunshine. At the doorway of the stables he spotted Collie. Lying around her were a half dozen pudgy puppies.

When a puppy came up to White Fang, Collie snarled a warning at him. Father and puppy touched noses. White Fang licked the puppy's face.

The gods clapped their hands, smiling and laughing. White Fang lay down, and the other puppies came. They played and tumbled over him. For a long time, he lay with half-shut, patient eyes, drowsing in the sun.